THE DAY HENRY MET A DOG

written and illustrated by
Gilly

One day, Henry met a dog.

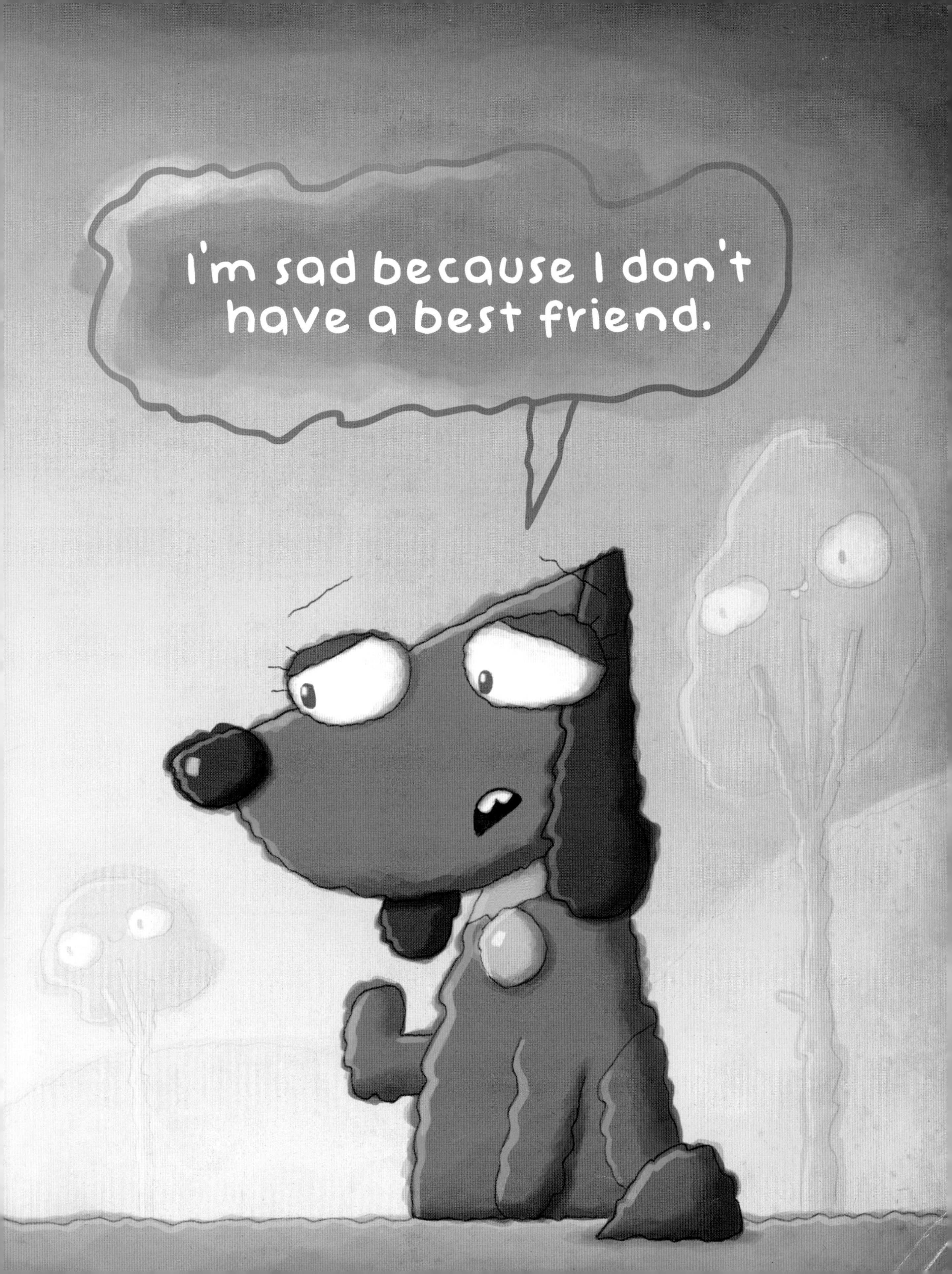
I'm sad because I don't have a best friend.

I wish I could find someone . . .

who makes me laugh,
who shares with me
and who plays with me.

Oh, I'll never find
a best friend around here.

That gives me a

We could become wildlife explorers.
And we could explore the jungle to find me a best friend.

Henry tells jokes, pulls faces
and makes Dog laugh.
Dog thinks Henry is hilarious.

Dog loves her adventure
in the jungle with Henry, but . . .

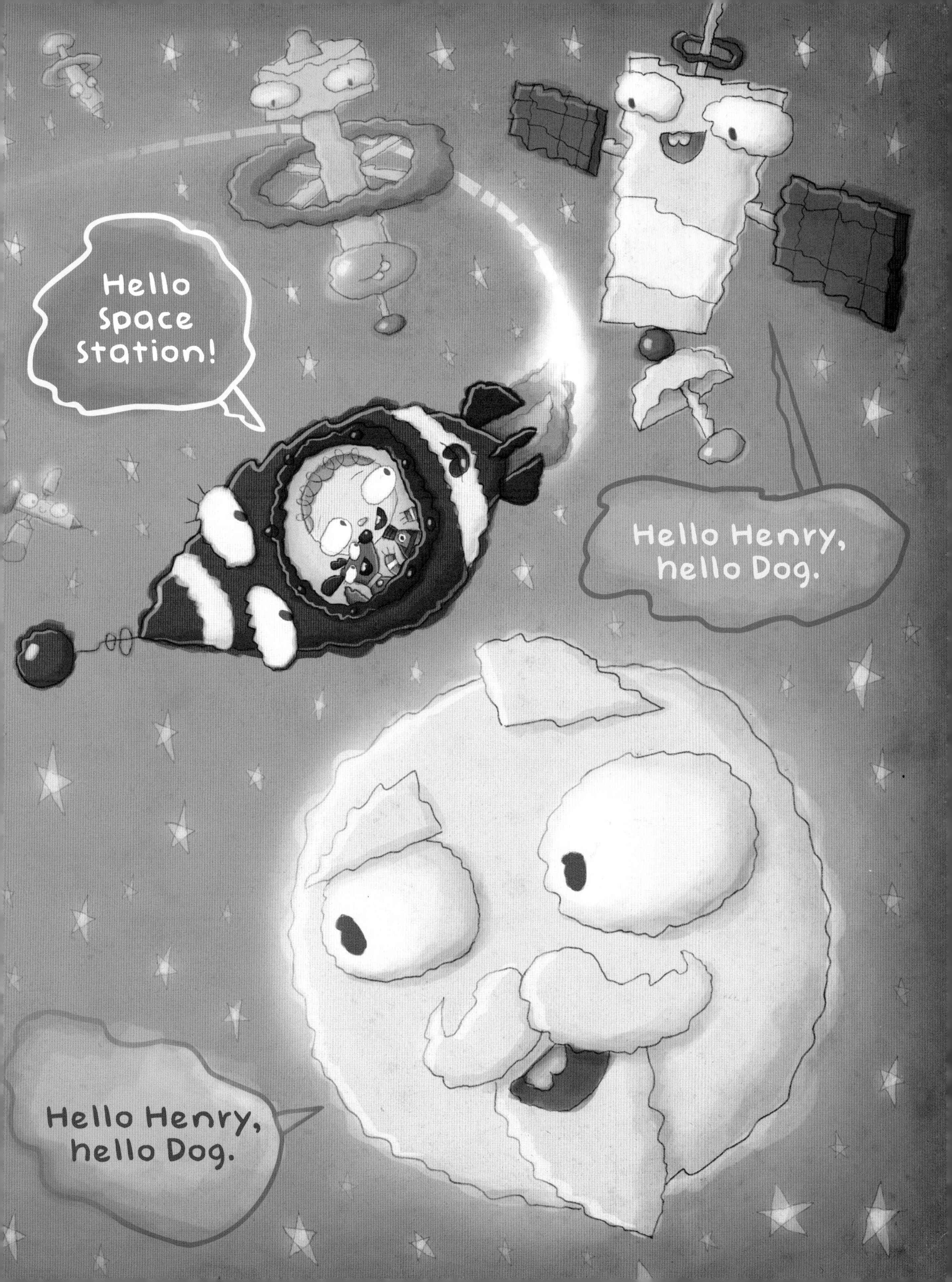

Dog is hungry, so Henry makes
a picnic on the moon, and shares
his favourite food with her.

Dog loves her adventure
in outer space with Henry, but . . .

We could become
deep sea divers.

Henry finds a treasure chest
at the bottom of the sea, and it's
filled with the most amazing things.

Toys + Games

Dog loves her adventure
under the sea with Henry, but . . .

But I'm sure you'll find someone

who makes you laugh,

who shares
with you

and who plays with you.

Just then
Dog realised something . . .

Hi, my name is Gilly. I live in Dublin with my lovely family, Josey Poo Poo Face, Henry Wenry, Rosie Purevoice and Tom the Tormentor.

I love drawing pictures and writing silly stories. Other things I love are Werther's Original, my completed Italia '90 Panini Sticker Book, the sauce they put into doner kebabs, me ma, me da, Al and Wen. But the thing I love the most, more than anything in the world, is getting the bins out just in time for collection.

Bye bye everyone, and be nice.

First published 2018 by The O'Brien Press Ltd,
12 Terenure Road East, Rathgar, Dublin 6, D06 HD27, Ireland
Tel: +353 1 4923333; Fax: +353 1 4922777
E-mail: books@obrien.ie
Website: www.obrien.ie
The O'Brien Press is a member of Publishing Ireland.

ISBN: 978-1-84717-999-9
Text and illustrations by Gilly 2018
'The Day Henry Met' is a trademark and copyright of Wiggleywoo Ltd
Licensed by Monster Entertainment
Copyright for book layout and design © The O'Brien Press Ltd
Inspired by the animation TV series 'The Day Henry Met' produced by
Wiggleywoo Ltd

10 9 8 7 6 5 4 3 2 1
23 22 21 20 19 18

Printed and bound in Drukarnia Skleniarz, Poland. The paper in this
book is produced using pulp from managed forests.

Published in
DUBLIN
UNESCO
City of Literature